The Great Big Parade

Written by Christine Ricci

Illustrated by Dave Aikins, Bob Roper, Zina Saunders, Steve Savitsky, and Victoria Miller

Louis Weber, C.E.O.
Publications International, Ltd.
7373 North Cicero Avenue, Lincolnwood, Illinois 60712
Ground Floor, 59 Gloucester Place, London W1U 8JJ

Customer Service: 1-800-595-8484 or customer_service@pilbooks.com

www.pilbooks.com

ISBN-13: 978-1-4127-8923-3
ISBN-10: 1-4127-8923-0

 publications international, ltd.

¡Hola! I'm Dora. Do you like parades? Today we're having a great big parade! Will you be in our parade? Great! Boots and I are going to march from my house all the way to town.

I hear hammering. Who has a hammer?
It's Tico! He's building a parade float for our
great big parade! What does Isa have? Oh!
Her wheelbarrow is full of flowers to decorate
the float! Isa and Tico are working together to
make a beautiful parade float!

Uh oh! There's the Troll Bridge.
The Grumpy Old Troll won't let us cross
his bridge until we answer his riddle.
    The Troll says, "This parade won't
get past me, unless you count the balloons
you see."

We have to count all the balloons.
How many balloons are there? Eight! Yay!
The Grumpy Old Troll says we can cross
his bridge. He loves parades! He's giving
a balloon to everyone in the parade!
Come march with us, Mr. Troll!

Uh oh! There's a river. I wonder how we can get our great big parade across the river. Explorer Stars can help! Do you see a star? It's Saltador the Super-Jumping Star! He can do a super jump to get the parade over the river! To tell him to jump, say *"isalta!"*

We're almost to Town. I think I hear Swiper! Do you see Swiper? There he is! Hey, Swiper isn't trying to swipe our stuff — he wants to join our parade!

And look! Swiper brought Special Parade
Stickers for everyone!
What a great surprise!

Oh no! A tire on our parade float got stuck in a hole. We need everyone to push the float out of the hole. Will you help us push? Say *"empujen."* Alright! We worked together to push the tire out of the hole. Great teamwork!

We're almost to Town! But which road do we need to take to get there? Can you tell which road is the right one? That's right! It's the road the red bird is on! Now we can take this parade straight through town! Everyone will get to enjoy the parade!

What a great day! Everyone worked together to help our parade get bigger and greater! It's the Biggest and Greatest Parade ever! We couldn't have had our great big parade without you! We make a great team! Thanks for helping!